Wheeler's Special Gift

Wheeler's

Special Gift

by Daniel Schantz

Art by Ned O.

STANDARD PUBLISHING
Cincinnati, Ohio
24-03952

Wheeler's Adventures

Wheeler's Deal

Wheeler's Big Catch

Wheeler's Ghost Town

Wheeler's Good Time

Wheeler's Big Break

Wheeler's Vacation

Wheeler's Freedom

Wheeler's Campaign

Wheeler's Treasure

Wheeler's Special Gift

Wheeler's Swap

Wheeler's Big Move

Library of Congress Cataloging in Publication Data

Schantz, Daniel.
    Wheeler's special gift.

    (Wheeler's adventures ; 10)
    Summary: During a hot, dry spell in July, the Wheeler family decides to celebrate Christmas and has a contest to see who can give the best Christmas gift.
    [1. Christmas—Fiction. 2. Family life—Fiction.]
I. Ostendorf, Edward, ill. II. Title. III. Series: Schantz, Daniel.
Wheeler's adventures ; 10.
PZ7.S3338Wj 1989   [Fic]   89-5912
ISBN 0-87403-572-4

Cover illustration by Richard D. Wahl

Copyright © 1989, The STANDARD PUBLISHING
   Company, Cincinnati, Ohio
A division of STANDEX INTERNATIONAL Corporation
Printed in U.S.A.

to Rick and Denise Willis,
and their little angels,
Ashlee and Lacey

Contents

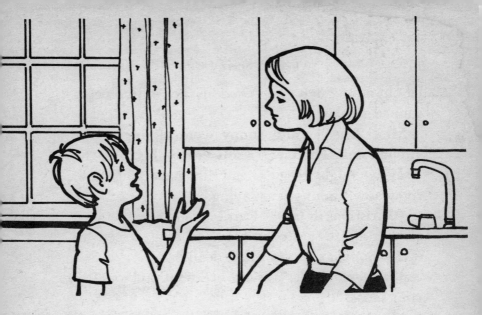

1 • A Wild Idea

A dust devil was headed straight for Earnest, but he didn't see it. Panting and puffing, he trudged up the driveway with an armload of books. His face was dripping with sweat, and his clean shirt was soaked from the heat of the July drought.

Just as he reached the porch steps, the little tornado swirled over him, dusting him with grit and dirt. He growled and sputtered and leaped up the steps.

Inside, Earnest plopped into a kitchen chair. He

let out a long sigh and wiped his face with an egg-stained napkin.

Mrs. Wheeler and Sonny were talking at the kitchen sink. There was a silly grin on his face. "So I say we ought to go ahead and have Christmas right now," Sonny was saying.

"Christmas in July?" Earnest yelled, with a look of horror. He scratched his head and crossed his eyes. "Sonny, you are brain dead."

Sonny scowled. "It's no crazier than some of your ideas."

Mr. Wheeler ambled into the kitchen, still dressed only in his P.J. bottoms. He dropped into a chair and yawned a huge yawn that seemed to last forever. Then he smacked his lips and said, "What's this about Christmas?"

Mrs. Wheeler combed his hair with her left hand and gave him a wake-up kiss. Then she reached for the calendar. "Well, Ralph, I was just looking at the calendar. Did you realize that our family won't be together for Christmas this year?"

Mr. Wheeler chomped into a doughnut and raised an eyebrow. "None of us? I know I won't be back from mechanic's school, but . . ."

"Right, and the boys promised to visit their cousin Andy in Florida, remember?"

"Hot dog!" Earnest sang out. "Christmas on the beach."

"At the Specific Ocean," Sonny added, but Earnest rolled his eyes.

"The Specific Ocean? You mean the Pacific. And it's not the Pacific anyhow, it's the Atlantic, so there. The Pacific is out in Utah."

Sonny looked hurt.

Mrs. Wheeler smiled and looked again at the calendar. "And I promised to help my sister in Indiana put on a Christmas program for the people at her rest home. That cuts me out."

Sonny reached for a doughnut. "So what's wrong with *my* idea?" he asked. "Let's just celebrate Christmas right now and get it over with. I could use some presents."

Earnest hissed. "You could use some new brain cells." He jumped up and ripped back the kitchen window curtain. "Does this look like Christmas to any of you?" His voice was gruff. "I mean, we are in the middle of a *drought*. The lawn is burnt up and the temperature is 95 degrees at . . . eight-thirty in the morning."

Sonny stiffened, and a stubborn look came over him. "What's that got to do with anything?" he yelled back.

Earnest let go of the curtain. "You've got to have snow to have Christmas," he fired back.

"Oh, yeah? Well, what do they do for Christmas in Africa, paint the ground white? And what about Australia and South America?"

"I'm with Earnest," Mr. Wheeler said. "It just wouldn't be the same without cold air and snow."

Mrs. Wheeler bristled. She sat up straight and crossed her arms. "Oh, I don't know about that," she said, icily. "I think maybe Sonny has something here. After all, there wasn't any snow when Jesus was born, was there?" She got up and wandered to the window, where she gazed out with a defiant look on her face. "Maybe Sonny is right. It's pretty sad if we can't celebrate Christmas unless we're freezing.

"In fact," Mrs. Wheeler added, "I think it would be a lot of fun to have a really, truly different kind of Christmas."

Earnest started to stomp out the door toward his room. "This is the most mouse-brained idea I've ever heard of."

"You're just jealous cause you didn't think of it," Sonny shouted after him. "And you're always too cheap to buy presents, anyway."

"I am not!" Earnest replied, stepping back into

the kitchen. "I just think it's a cornball idea. What are the neighbors gonna think if we put up a Christmas tree in July?"

Mr. Wheeler nodded. "Mrs. Collins will call the police, and they will haul us all off to the Nut Hut."

Mrs. Wheeler laughed. "I can't believe you guys. Come on, lighten up. If we want to put up a tree in July, who cares? I mean, really. It's a free country. Besides, who says we even have to put up a tree?"

Earnest slumped into a chair. "I don't like Christmas anyhow. As far as I'm concerned we can just cancel it altogether. It's always the same old thing. We eat too much, listen to dumb songs and buy a bunch of presents we don't need and can't afford."

Mrs. Wheeler put her hands on her hips and whipped her blonde hair back out of her face. "That's just my point, Earnest. Maybe Christmas has lost its meaning because of those trappings. Since there aren't any of the usual trappings in July, maybe celebrating in July would give it a different feel."

"Yeah, like *hot*," Earnest interrupted.

"Tell you what," his mother continued. "Let's

do something truly different." She blinked, thinking about the possibilities.

"Like what?" Sonny asked.

Mrs. Wheeler paused. "Maybe we ought to leave that up to all of you." She blinked again and added, "I challenge you all to see who can give the most creative and unusual Christmas gift."

Earnest rolled his eyes and reached for some ice from the icemaker. "How about an ice storm? That would be creative." He popped a chunk in his mouth.

Mrs. Wheeler reached again for the calendar. "Let's see. Today is July 15. What do you say we appoint July 25th as our Christmas Day instead of December 25?"

"I don't get it," Sonny said. "What kind of creative gift are you talking about? I don't have a lotta money."

Mrs. Wheeler stroked her chin. "I'm not sure," she replied. "It could be something you *make* . . . something you *do* for someone . . . something you *buy* . . . almost anything." She reached for a sheet of paper in a drawer and began taping it to the wall by the phone. "Whatever you decide to give, write it up here, and on Christmas Eve we will decide whose is best."

"Who is gonna be the judge?" Sonny asked. "And what's the prize?"

"Yeah," Earnest agreed.

"How about Cherry? I know she would be fair. And no prize except the honor. If you got a prize it wouldn't be giving, it would be trading."

Mr. Wheeler rinsed his mouth with orange juice. He pulled up from the table and shuffled toward the door. "I still say it's a dorky idea," he muttered to himself. "Christmas in July? What next? Easter in January? We could get arrested. We'll all melt in this heat."

Earnest followed his father out to the garage. Halfway, his father paused and smashed a clump of dried grass with his shoe. He shook his head slowly and seriously. "This drought is getting very serious."

"Pretty bad?" Earnest asked.

His father gazed up at the sun. "Drought is a very dangerous thing. Lots of elderly people will die."

A siren in the distance seemed to prove his point. He went on. "See how dry this grass is? It doesn't take much to set this afire. Fields, trees, outbuildings . . . it can all go up in smoke. Thousands of dollars gone in a flash."

"What about farmers?" Earnest asked. "What do they do?"

"They *suffer*, that's what. Every time we have a drought, several more farmers go out of business. Food prices go up. Small towns die. The drought affects my business, too."

"The car repair business?"

Mr. Wheeler nodded. "Trucks. When farmers are hurting, they put off repairs on their cars and trucks. That hurts me."

"I feel sorry for the farmers," Earnest said quietly. "It must be awful to depend on the weather for a living."

"Well, the farmers understand nature. They don't expect to have a good year every year." He reached out and caught a grasshopper that leaped in front of him. He held it where Earnest could see its big head sticking out of his fingers. Brown juice oozed from the bug's mouth.

"More bad news." he said. "Drought causes the insects to multiply. What the drought doesn't get, the 'hoppers and spider mites will finish off."

There was a noise from the back porch. Sonny bounded out the door singing, "I'm dreaming of a wet Christmas . . . just like the one that Noah knew . . ." He leaped over the porch railing and skipped away toward his workshop.

"What are you up to?" Earnest asked, as Sonny swished past him.

"Gonna build something," Sonny announced. "Something for Christmas." He disappeared into the garage.

Earnest grinned at his father, and his father grinned back. "Leave it to Sonny to start things off with a bang," he said, chuckling to himself.

2 • Locked In

Mr. Wheeler was bolting new license plates on a car when a shadow fell across the open garage door. He glanced up and saw a large sheet of wood paneling moving across the doorway by itself.

"Can I use some of this stuff?" a voice said from behind the paneling. Sonny peered around the edge of the board.

"Where did you get it?" Mr. Wheeler asked.

"It was stacked alongside the garage."

Mr. Wheeler squinted at the board. "I guess so. I don't think I'm saving it for anything special."

The wood moved away. Sonny carried five sheets of the wood out under the big maple tree so he could work in the shade. Already he was drenched in sweat, so he peeled off his shirt. As he did so, someone tickled him from behind.

"Hey! Quit! Oh, hi, Cherry."

Cherry was wearing an oversized yellow sun dress and holding a white sun umbrella in her hand. "Whatcha doin'?" she asked, sweetly, blinking her big green eyes and playing with her red hair.

Sonny plucked a pencil from behind his ear and gazed at the sheet of wood. "Don't know for sure," he said, "Trying to make a manger set, but I don't know . . ."

"A manger? In the summertime?"

Sonny scratched his head with the pencil point. "It's hard to explain. How do you make a wise man? I can't draw, can you?"

Cherry shook her head. "Why don't you lie down on the board and I'll trace around you."

Sonny mouth fell open. "Great idea!" He tossed her the pencil and dropped to the ground on top of the sheet of wood.

"How's this?"

"Put your hands down at your side."

Cherry guided the pencil around Sonny's skinny body, starting at his left ear.

"Awwk! That tickles. Hurry!"

"Hold still. Just a little more. There, all done."

Sonny leaped up and looked at the tracing. "Hey, not bad except for the knees. Now all it needs is a face. I can do that later."

With his father's electric scroll saw he cut out the outline of himself. Then he stood it up against the tree and admired it as he told Cherry about the Christmas-in-July idea. "So," he added, "I'm going to make decorations as my gift, starting with this manger set."

The two of them traced two more wise men and cut them out.

"Now, I need a camel . . ."

Cherry started to walk away. "Uh . . . I have to go help my grandma with the laundry."

"Cherry! Don't leave me now! Come back!"

But already she was skipping down the drive. "See ya," she called back.

Sonny stared at the big sheet of wood and sighed. "I don't know how to make a camel." But he knelt over the board and began to draw, starting with the legs. He added a two-hump body then a long, crooked neck. Last, he tried three times to draw a camel's head. Then he stood up to admire his work.

"Oh, croak. It looks like a deformed dinosaur. Oh, well, it's gonna have to do."

An hour later Sonny was cutting out a donkey when his scroll saw blade snapped with a loud *ping!*

"Awww, rats. I was almost done, too." He trudged to the garage, looking for his father.

"Dad, you got any more of these saw blades?"

His father was wearing his welding mask, which made him look like someone from a Star Wars movie. "In the trunk of our car, in the tool box," he mumbled through the mask. From his pocket he fished a key and tossed it to Sonny. "Watch out for that trunk lid. It doesn't stay up by itself. You could hurt your head."

"What?" Sonny hollered back over his shoulder.

"I said, watch out for the trunk lid."

Sonny shook his head. "Sorry, I can't understand you through that mask." He trotted away to the family car, which was sitting in the drive.

Sonny twisted the key and the trunk lid sprang up. It barely stayed open by itself. He looked all around inside the trunk, then spotted the red tool box deep inside next to some to oil cans. He stretched out to grab it, but he couldn't reach it, so he climbed in. With both hands he clutched the box, then turned around.

All at once the trunk lid dropped slowly and silently, but surely to the latch. It closed tightly with a big *click*.

"Uh-oh," Sonny muttered. He pushed up on the lid, but it didn't budge. "Double uh-oh," he said to himself in the pitch black of the closed trunk. "I gotta get out of here. It's hot in here."

He leaned his back against the lid and pushed with all his might, but nothing happened. His

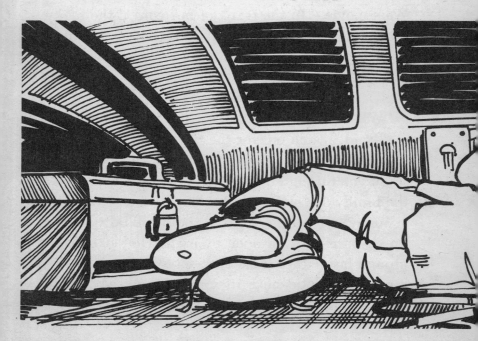

hands felt around the trunk floor, reaching, clutching for something, anything that might help. At last he found a tire wrench and he slid it into the trunk latch and pried up with all his might.

Whang! the wrench snapped, but the lid was still locked. Already his arms and face were slippery with sweat, and his breath felt like fire in his face. Every time he moved he bumped into something, and it seemed like the trunk walls were closing in on him. He began to whimper.

"Maybe I can go through the back of the seat

into the car," he said, with desperation in his voice. He shoved and pried and pounded and tore at the seat back, but nothing budged. Now his heart was thundering in his chest and he was breathing like a runner on the last lap.

"I gotta get out of here! I gotta get out of here! I gotta get out!" Once again he threw himself against the lid with all his might, but he only managed to slice his back on the sharp metal edges.

He collapsed on the floor of the trunk, gasping for breath. Then he began to shout at the top of his lungs. "Dad! Help! Anybody! Help! I'm in the trunk, help!" He listened for sounds of someone, but nothing happened. He rolled over and sobbed into his arms.

Meanwhile, the rest of the family was just sitting down at the table for lunch. Mr. Wheeler was reading the newspaper and Earnest was figuring something on his hand calculator.

"Where's Sonny?" he asked, only halfway interested.

Mrs. Wheeler slid a platter of hot dogs in front of him. "He's been working out under the tree all morning," she said. She stepped to the door and hollered out, "Sonny! Lunch! Hot dogs! Come on, right now!"

There was no answer. "Well, when he gets hungry enough, he'll be along."

After the blessing, Mr. Wheeler glanced once more at his paper. "Say, Earnest, isn't this a friend of yours? Louie Magee?"

"Maggot? Let me see."

"It says here he just got out of the hospital."

"Maggot? In the hospital? For what?"

"Hyperthermia."

"What's that?"

"Heat stroke."

Earnest shook his head sadly. "That poor kid. I feel sorry for him."

"Who is he?" Mrs. Wheeler asked.

"Don't you remember? He was the only kid that showed up at Sonny's pizza sale. He's real fat and he has—"

"Don't say fat, say large."

"Okay, large and fat. He has big lips . . ."

"That black kid?"

Earnest shook his head. "No, you know who I mean. The one who always says, 'Bingo.' It's his favorite word."

"Oh, him! Now I know who you mean. Why do you feel sorry for him?"

"Cause. He flunked out of school this year.

Flunked it *cold*. He got kicked out once before 'cause he had lice."

Mrs. Wheeler shuddered and clutched her hair. "I was just about to say that maybe you ought to call on him and see if you can cheer him up, but maybe that's not such a good idea."

Suddenly the kitchen door swung open and in dragged Sonny. His hair was matted down and dripping sweat. His face and belly were deeply scratched and bleeding, and his pants were torn at the waist.

"Sonny!" his mother gasped. "What on earth happened to you? Where have you been? What's wrong?"

Sonny dropped into his chair, breathing hard. He grabbed his water glass and poured it over his own head. Then he reached for Earnest's glass and chugged the entire glassful in three swallows. For a while he just sat there gasping. Then, between gasps, he whispered, "Let's just say I've been to a lock-in."

3 • Open Door

The wind blew hot and moist in his face as Earnest pedaled his bike out McKinley Road. In a few minutes he had to stop to rest, and he plucked some blackberries by the fence to quench his thirst. Then he rode on.

At last he braked beside a rusty, crooked mailbox and squinted to read the name on it.

"Magee," he mumbled. "This must be the place."

When he turned and looked across the road his mouth fell open. "What in the . . ."

In the middle of a weedy lot sat a small mobile home that tilted sharply to one side. Strewn all around the home were countless pieces of junk and trash: a broken lawnmower, a rusty clothes washer, an old pickup truck, two gutted televisions and an old refrigerator.

Earnest shuffled slowly toward the mobile home, not quite certain what to think or do. He weaved around a child's swimming pool filled with old car batteries. Carefully he tiptoed through a mound of broken windows, climbed over a pile of firewood and dodged a broken picnic table. When he neared the steps, a flock of hens squawked and scattered into the weeds in front of him. A big, lazy dog opened his eyes and looked at Earnest, then slowly closed them and went back to sleep.

Earnest stepped on the first porch step and the board swung up and smacked him in the elbow.

"Ouch!" He rubbed his elbow and took the rest of the steps in one leap, so as not to take any chances. He started to knock on the door, but there was no door. He looked down and saw the door lying in the grass at the base of the home.

"Hello!" he called out, knocking on the door frame at the same time.

"Hello! Anyone home? It's me, Earnest. Hello?"

No one answered. He peeked in the doorway, then tiptoed inside. "This must be the kitchen," he mumbled to himself.

The kitchen table was piled with old dishes and food was still on the plates. Flocks of noisy flies were holding banquets at each plate. A mousetrap was sitting on the table, and there was a dead mouse in it.

Earnest loosened his shirt. "Sure is hot in here." A terrible odor hit him in the face, and he gasped, putting his hand over his mouth.

He peered down the hallway. "Anybody home?" he called out again.

No answer.

"I wonder if I should wait a while or go home?" he asked himself. He noticed there were two broken chairs at the kitchen table and no other furniture except for a television and an old stove with strings of spaghetti stuck to its door.

A shadow fell across the doorway. "Hi!" a strong, cheerful voice sang out. "How ya doin'?"

Earnest whirled around and saw Maggot smiling through black and missing teeth. He was wearing a pair of cutoffs and nothing else. His big, rounded belly looked ready to burst, and his legs bowed so badly they seemed like they would break any minute.

"Great to see you, guy!" Maggot sang out, happily.

Earnest blushed. "I . . . I didn't mean to just walk into your house . . . I . . ."

Maggot laughed. "Hey! There's no door," he said, pointing to the open doorway. He reached for a box of cereal and began stuffing his mouth with dry frosted flakes. "Want some?" he said, holding the box out to Earnest.

Earnest shook his head.

Maggot went on crunching the flakes and looking at Earnest blankly. A big flake was clinging to his lower lip, dancing up and down as he chewed. "Have a seat," Maggot said, pointing to a broken kitchen chair.

Slowly, carefully Earnest sat down and turned his face away from the smelly table. A fly suddenly landed on his lip and Earnest sputtered it way.

Maggot sat on a pile of old clothes, trying in vain to cross his legs, Indian style. "So, what brings you way out here?" he asked between chews.

Earnest scratched his head, then his stomach, as

if he was beginning to itch all over. "Well, I heard you were in the hospital."

Maggot nodded. He reached for a stale, warm glass of orange juice and poured it down his throat with gurgling, choking sounds. "I was out in the yard, you know, trying to move that old firewood outta the way, and bingo, I went out like a light."

He laughed and added, "Woke up in a hospital bed." Maggot wiped juice from his lips with the back of his hand, then wiped his hand under his armpit. "Sure good to be outta that place, let me tell ya."

There was a rustling sound in the next room down the hall.

"Where's your mom and dad?" Earnest asked, timidly.

Maggot let out a long, low belch. "Dad's gone to work. Got a new job over at the lumber yard." He shook his head and belched again. "But it won't last. It never does."

"What do you mean?"

Maggot shrugged. "Dad has this bad temper, you know? I say it's the drinking. Whenever he gets upset, he just blows up, and bingo that's the end of the job."

"Oh, I see."

"Mom is . . . well, no tellin' where she is." He tapped his finger on the side of his head. "Mom is . . . you know?"

Earnest looked puzzled. "She's . . ."

"She spends most of her time picking up pop cans or over at the city landfill." He held out the box of frosted flakes. "Are you sure you don't want some of these?"

Earnest shook his head.

Maggot peered into the cereal box.

"Good thing. They're all gone." He pitched the box into the corner and dusted his hands.

Earnest looked all around the room. "Where is all your furniture?" he asked meekly.

Again there was a rustling sound in the other room, like something crawling through a box.

Maggot staggered to his feet and glanced down the hall. "The bank took all our furniture," he said, calmly. "We use these clothes for chairs. People are always bringing us used clothes. Clothes, clothes, clothes. Who needs clothes in this weather, anyhow? Why don't they ever bring us ice cream?" Maggot bent over and picked up an old, scraggly broom. He laid it on his shoulder and turned toward the hallway. All at once he took off running and screaming down the hall.

"Wrraaaaaaa!" he shrieked, slamming the broom up and down on the floor. *"Get out of here, you stupid animal! Out! Out! Out!"*

Suddenly a big, fat raccoon wriggled between Maggot's legs and headed straight for Earnest. Earnest staggered back and fell off his chair. The coon stared at Earnest for a second, then turned and bounded out the doorway and into the weeds.

Maggot tossed the broom after him. "Stupid coon gets in here every day. I don't understand it."

Earnest righted his broken chair and sat back down. Maggot sprawled out on his pile of rags.

"I . . . I was sorry to hear you flunked out of school," Earnest said. "It won't be the same without you in class."

Maggot stopped chewing and grew quiet, his eyes darting here and there. For a while he said nothing. There was only the sound of his heavy breathing. He seemed to be deep in thought. He picked up a broken watch and played with it.

"I didn't mean to embarrass you," Earnest said, softly.

Maggot looked up at Earnest with clouded eyes. "It's okay. I'm not proud of it." His voice cracked. "But me and books don't get along so hot, you know?"

Earnest nodded. "What's the problem? Can I help? I mean, school comes easy for me."

Maggot turned his head toward the wall and muttered to himself. "I ain't no good at all that reading stuff. I *want* to read, but I start it and bingo, I just lose it."

"Maybe I could help," Earnest suggested.

Maggot looked up at Earnest with despair in his eyes. "I wish somebody could help. I don't want to be like Dad and Mom." He shook his head and played with the watch. "I mean, don't get me wrong, I love my parents and all that, but . . . well, I wanna *be* something when I grow up."

Earnest stood up. "Well, then let's do something about it!" he said. "You're smart, you can learn. I'll help you." He looked around the room. "Bring me a book."

Maggot shrugged. "Ain't got no books. I checked some outta the library once, but Mom threw them away. Can't get no more, now."

"Okay, a magazine will do."

"Ain't got none."

"Newspaper?"

Maggot shook his head.

Earnest looked around the room desperately. He reached out and grabbed a frozen pizza box, then

plopped down beside Maggot.

"Okay, this will do. Let's get started." He turned the box over and held it up for Maggot to see the printed instructions.

"Can you read any of these words?" Earnest asked, pointing to the directions for cooking.

Maggot clutched the box in his fat fingers and held it close to his face. He licked a bead of sweat off his upper lip and began reading.

"Re . . . re . . . re . . ."

"Remove," Earnest coached him.

"Remove from buh . . . buh . . . box . . ."

"Good! Keep goin'."

"Remove from box and puh . . . puh-lace in o . . . o . . . o . . ."

"Oven."

"Place in oven, yeah, that's it. Place in oven, stupid."

Earnest smiled at him. "You're doin' fine, Mag, real fine. And you're *not* stupid."

Maggot grinned with his yellow-stained teeth. Earnest caught a strong whiff of bad breath.

4 • Odd Things

Ralph and Joyce Wheeler were reading in bed when Sonny and Earnest traipsed into the room, dressed for bed.

"It's too hot in our room," Sonny whined. "We can't sleep."

The two of them lounged on the bed at their parents' feet. Earnest opened a book and began reading.

"There's a fan in the hall closet," Mr. Wheeler said. "And if you just lie real still you won't be so hot."

Sonny propped his head on his hands and wrinkled his brow. "Mom, what are we gonna do for Christmas Eve? The usual dinner and opening presents?"

His mother put down her magazine. "I'm not sure. I want this Christmas to really different." She looked away, as if trying to picture Christmas Eve in her mind. "I think my gift to the family will be a very special Christmas Eve dinner. Something . . . something truly unusual."

Earnest peered over his book. "Just so it's not fish," he growled.

"Fish?" his mother asked. "Why would I want to serve fish?"

Earnest held up his book. "I've been reading about Christmas in other lands. In lots o' places they serve fish. Let's see, Sweden, Holland . . . in Germany they serve a big fat carp. Yug!"

Mrs. Wheeler smiled. "I can remember when my grandma used to fix oysters every Christmas. Oysters, turnips, cabbage . . . and headcheese."

"What's headcheese?" Sonny asked, with wide eyes.

"You don't want to know."

Earnest flipped a few pages in his book. "It says here that in Spain they serve a stew made of pig's feet, bacon, lard, garlic, and mutton. What's mutton?"

"That's lamb."

"And in Eth . . . ethi . . . op . . ."

"Ethiopia?"

"Yeah, in Ethiopia they eat raw meat. I think I'm gonna be sick."

Mr. Wheeler reached for his alarm clock and set it for seven. "I still say it's going to seem mighty odd having Christmas in this heat."

Earnest flipped back a few pages in his book. "Maybe not so odd," he said. "Did you know that in 1888 our country had the warmest Christmas on record?"

"Like, how warm?" Sonny asked.

"Well, in New York City it was 102 degrees. There were still flowers growing and robins on the lawns. It says people were playing croquet— whatever that is—and serving Christmas dinner like a picnic."

Mrs. Wheeler's face lit up. "No kidding? A picnic?" She played with her hair and smiled to herself.

Earnest nodded. "That's nothing. In South America Christmas comes at the hottest time of the year. They sell ice in little booths along the streets. And in Australia they exchange gifts at breakfast, before it gets too hot to enjoy it."

"That's interesting."

"What do they do for decorations?" Sonny wanted to know. "I'm doing decorations as my present to the family. I need some ideas."

Earnest fanned a few pages in his book. "Decorations . . . I saw something on that . . . okay, here. In lots of countries they decorate with flowers. Even the tree is covered with flowers."

"Flowers? At Christmas? No way."

Earnest pointed to the page as proof. "And you know how we hang up Christmas stockings to be filled with candy?"

"Don't tell me," Mr. Wheeler said. "They hang up their underwear."

"Ralph!"

"Nope. Shoes. In Mexico, anyway. And you know how we put out cookies and milk for Santa?"

Sonny nodded. "They put out raw fish, right?"

"No, not fish. In Brazil they put out boxes of straw or grass for the wise men's camels. And . . . in many countries they celebrate Christmas the way we celebrate the Fourth of July, with fireworks and noisemakers."

"Oh, sure," Mrs. Wheeler chimed in. "They still do that down south in our own country. Grandma used to buy us fireworks at Christmas. I think she said the custom started in England, as a way to drive off evil spirits and witches."

Mr. Wheeler pulled his pillow up over his head and said in a muffled voice, "I wish someone would drive away the evil spirits in my bed. C'mon, you guys, let's get some Z's, okay?"

Mrs. Wheeler jerked the pillow away from him. "But Ralph, you haven't said what you are going to give me for Christmas."

Ralph sat up in bed. He bared his teeth and twisted his big hands into claws and let out a long growl. "For Kleesmas, I yam go-ing to *keel* some-one for keeping me a-wake! Ruaaaaaaaaaaaaaarr-rrr!"

The boys leaped off the bed with a yelp and streaked off to their rooms with squeals of terror.

Mrs. Wheeler stroked the hair out of her husband's eyes and kissed him on the nose. "I'm not afraid of monsters," she said, then added, "Ralphie, Sweetheart, don't you think maybe we could get a new car for Christmas, huh, Sweetie Pie Honey Bunch?"

He shook his head. "I wish. But we just don't

have the money. Have you seen the prices on new cars?"

"But, Ralph, we *sell* cars! There are thirty-five beautiful cars out there on your lot, and we drive the worst car in town. The upholstery is falling off. There are holes in the floor. I'm ashamed to be seen in that thing."

"I'm trying to fix it," he mumbled, growing sleepier. "Just give me a little time." He buried his head under the pillow and drifted off to sleep.

In the middle of the night, Mrs. Wheeler staggered out of bed and padded down the stairs to the kitchen for a drink of water.

She drank one glassful, then refilled the glass to take back to her room. When she turned and started back upstairs, she froze in her tracks. The glass dropped from her hands and shattered at her feet. Her face turned white, and she let out a long scream.

Instantly lights came on. Mr. Wheeler came crashing down the stairs, and the boys peered from their rooms, then rushed to her side. They found her sitting at the dining room table, clutching her throat and breathing rapidly and deeply.

"Joyce, what's wrong? What is it?" Mr. Wheeler knelt beside her.

Without a word she pointed to the living room. There, profiled against the living room window stood an enormous dinosaur-shaped camel and a donkey that looked like a tall dog with rabbit's ears.

"Uh-oh," Sonny muttered. "I think I'm in trouble."

Mrs. Wheeler stood up, still trembling. "What on earth are those *creatures* doing in my living room!"

Sonny pranced around nervously and stammered. "Mom I'm sorry. I didn't think. I had to bring 'em inside to paint 'em. It was just too hot to paint 'em outdoors, honest."

She looked at him in disbelief.

Sonny stooped to pick up pieces of glass, and Mr. Wheeler joined him. Earnest tromped back to his room.

"Mom, I promise I'll have 'em outta here first thing in the morning. I'll paint 'em in the garage."

"I *know* you will," she warned. "I *know* you will." She hobbled up the stairs to bed.

5 • Taking Shape

Sonny plopped the wise men down on the garage floor for painting.

"I'm warning you," his father called from the office. "I want those out of there by ten o'clock. I've got cars coming in."

"No sweat, Dad. This will be dry in twenty minutes."

Cherry held the paint can as Sonny sloshed the yellow paint on the wooden men and animals.

"How come you're using yellow?" Cherry asked meekly.

"It's all I got," Sonny explained. Already his long arms were splotched with yellow, and his big shoes were dotted with drips.

When the figures were about dry, Sonny and Cherry hauled them outside and leaned them against the garage.

"Do you think people driving by can see these okay?" Sonny asked.

Cherry looked around and nodded. "Sure, but the wise men don't have any faces," she pointed out.

Sonny scratched his head. "Yeah, I guess you're right. But I'll fix that." He disappeared into the office and soon bounded back with a big felt marker in his hand.

"What do wise men's faces look like?" he asked. He twisted his face into a serious look. "How's this?" he mumbled, without moving his lips.

Cherry started to giggle. "You don't look wise, you look stupid!" She studied the wooden people, then said, "Why don't you just make them look *happy?* People should be happy at Christmas."

Sonny shrugged. "Why not?" He popped open the marker and slowly began drawing big smiles on the faces, with lots of teeth.

Cherry giggled louder and louder, with each

stroke of his pen, until she was almost out of control.

Sonny drew straight lips on the animals, then added large, round eyes and long noses. Finally, he topped the wise men with curly hair.

Cherry wiped tears of laughter from her eyes. She groaned and held her stomach. "Ooooh, please don't make me laugh any more. It hurts."

Sonny paced back and forth, looking over his work. "Lookin' good," he decided. "Lookin' real good." He wiped sweat from his forehead and studied them once more. "Now all they need is some clothes. They look kinda naked."

While Sonny and Cherry were cleaning up their paints and brushes, Earnest was sitting at the kitchen table looking through some books. His mother returned from the store and plopped her shopping sacks on the table.

"Whatcha got, Mom?" Earnest asked, peering into the sacks. Gently but firmly she shoved his face back out of the way.

"Keep your big eyes to yourself," she warned.

Earnest grinned. "Ah-hah! Christmas presents, right?" He went back to sorting his books, putting some of them into a cardboard box and some into a paper sack.

"Got some new books?" his mother asked.

Earnest nodded. "Not exactly. These are for Maggot. My Christmas present to him."

"Oh? Isn't he the kid who flunked out of school?"

"Yep. I think it's 'cause he can't read well. I'm gonna teach him."

"Well, now, I think that's using your head . . . *and* your heart."

When Earnest had all the books packed in the box, he filled the leftover space with three bottles: a bottle of mouthwash, some deodorant, and a jar of men's cologne.

Earnest toted the box of books out to his bicycle and wriggled it into his bike basket. As he started to pedal away, he caught sight of Sonny's manger scene. He pushed the bike over to the garage for a better look. There he stood, shaking his head in disbelief.

"*Yellow* wise men with *smiling* faces?"

Sonny glared at him. "What's wrong with that? It's no worse than your face."

Again Earnest shook his head, then turned to leave. "Haven't you forgotten one small detail?" he asked, putting his foot on the pedal.

"What?"

"Like the baby Jesus, that's what."

Sonny blinked. "Oh, yeah. I'll get to that."

Once more Earnest shook his head, "At least get rid of those stupid smiling faces. Please! Give us all a break."

When Earnest was gone, Sonny looked again at his wise men. Lines of doubt formed on his forehead. "Maybe he's right," he muttered to himself. "Maybe the smiles are a bit much."

He lumbered into the house and sat down on the floor by the magazine rack. For a few minutes he thumbed through magazines, looking for large, "wise" faces. At last he had found three serious faces—one a movie star and two from electric razor ads. He ripped them out, then carefully cut around them with scissors.

On his way out of the house he found a cardboard box in the pantry to use for a manger. Then he reached for the phone.

"Hello, Mrs. Pepper? Can I talk to Cherry? . . . Cherry? Sonny. Listen, you know that manger set I'm making? Well, I have a problem. No, I need a baby Jesus for the manger. You got any dolls? . . . Well, bring it over. . . . Sure, that will work all right. Thanks. See ya."

Sonny tripped outside to his manger set. He laid

the figures down on the grass and pasted the serious faces on the wise men, on top of the smiling faces. Then he stood them back up. "Well," he said to himself, "I like the smiles better, but I guess Earnest is right."

For lunch, Mrs. Wheeler ordered a bucket of chicken and served it in the garage office. "It's too hot to cook," she explained, passing around the big bucket full of crunchy chicken pieces.

Mr. Wheeler said the blessing, then added a special plea for rain. The four of them lounged around on boxes and chairs, chewing chicken and slurping soda. Earnest was thumbing through a Christmas storybook.

"Dad," he said after a while, "How come they use such big words in the Christmas story? What does 'espoused' mean?"

"It means Joseph was engaged to marry her."

"Oh. Well, how about 'great with child?'"

"It means she was pregnant," Sonny interrupted. "Anybody knows that."

"Why didn't they just say she was pregnant?"

Mr. Wheeler swallowed a mouthful of chicken. "Oh, I don't know, I kinda like 'great with child' myself. It sounds poetic, you know? 'Pregnant' sounds like a disease."

"Ralph! It does not!"

Earnest looked back at the book. "What's this mean—'the days were accomplished.'"

"It means she was as fat as they get," Sonny blurted out. His mother glared at him.

"What's this about 'swaddling clothes'? What are swaddling clothes?"

Mrs. Wheeler wiped her lips with a napkin and cleared her throat. "Swaddling clothes? Oh, they were something like bandages. See, they didn't have cribs like ours, so they wrapped babies up like mummies so they couldn't roll out of bed."

"Poor kids," Sonny observed. "Starting life as a mummy. Chewee."

"It also helped keep their spine straight," his mother explained. "So it would develop right. And because the baby couldn't flail around, it didn't get so chafed and sore."

"Whatsamatter, didn't they have baby powder?"

"Well, yes. They used olive oil, but . . ."

Sonny scratched his head. "What if the baby had to . . . you know, do something?"

"Then they just unwrapped it and cleaned it."

Sonny chuckled to himself. "I can just hear Mom in the middle of the night. 'Ralph, the baby is crying. It's your turn to unwrap it. And don't forget to wrap it back up.'"

Earnest looked deep in thought. "Too bad they didn't have Pampers back then. If you owned the company you coulda made a fortune. I can just see the commercials. 'Don't swaddle your baby. Pamper him.'"

Sonny moaned. "Oh, Earnest, you're so lame."

Earnest stiffened. "Not as lame as someone who uses a Ziggy doll for the Christ child."

"Don't knock it," Sonny snapped back. "It's all I could find."

Mr. Wheeler stood up and stretched. He turned and strolled back into the garage, but over his shoulder he said, "I don't want any of you hanging around this garage, you understand?"

"What's chewing on him?" Sonny asked.

Mrs. Wheeler wrinkled her brow. "I don't know. I think he's been working on some kind of secret project out there. He's been working late almost every night for a month. Very mysterious, if you ask me."

6 • A Big Hug

When Earnest reached Maggot's mobile home, Maggot was sitting on the trailer steps, feeding the big coon. When Maggot saw Earnest coming toward him, he put his forefinger to his lips, warning Earnest to be quiet.

Earnest slowly set down his box of books and tiptoed closer and closer until he was standing right beside Maggot. He watched as Maggot reached into a bucket of water and pulled out a small, pinkish crawdad with tiny, restless pincers. The coon grabbed for it with two miniature paws that looked like human hands.

Maggot turned slowly, quietly toward Earnest and whispered, "I couldn't get rid of him, so I decided to make a friend of him."

Earnest watched in awe as the coon peeled and nibbled the crawdad like a hungry child chewing on jelly beans.

"I call him the Lone Ranger, because of his mask," Maggot whispered.

Earnest grinned with his eyes. "He looks so human," he whispered back.

"I know. Coons are really smart." He winked and added, "Smarter than some people I know." He rolled his eyes.

Earnest suddenly brushed a fly from his nose, and the quick motion startled the coon. With a jerk it turned and scampered off into the weeds.

"Who was that masked man?" Earnest quipped.

Maggot giggled, then stood up and motioned for Earnest to follow him. "I'll show you something else," he promised. He pulled himself up the steps, twisted through the doorway and clomped down the hallway. Earnest clipped along behind him.

Maggot stopped beside a big pile of clothes under the window. He reached down and slowly lifted an old red dress with his thick fingers. There was a squeaking sound, then Earnest saw two baby coons huddled together.

"Well, look at that!" Earnest said, cheerfully. "They look so *neat*, like little kittens dressed up for trick or treat."

Maggot's face beamed. "I call this one Batman and this one Foster Grant. Here, Foster, c'mon, time to eat." He handed the baby coon a tiny crawdad, but the coon only sniffed it.

"I don't think he's ready for solid food," Maggot said.

Earnest petted one of the coons very gently, then Maggot slowly lowered the dress back over them. "I think they need sleep more than meat," Maggot observed. "You know how babies are. They sleep and eat and stink, but mostly sleep."

Maggot wallowed down the hall to the kitchen, picking up a box of pretzels off the counter. "You want somethin' to eat?" he asked.

Earnest started to reach in the box, then decided to peek inside first. Satisfied, he pulled out one broken pretzel. "Just one, thanks."

"What brings you out in this heat?" Maggot mumbled through a big mouthful of salty, dry pretzel.

"I brought you something," Earnest said. "Wait here." He slid out the door and soon came back with his box of books. A chicken feather floated out of the box when he clunked it on the floor. Earnest looked at the kitchen table, which was still covered with dishes and food.

"Can we clear this off?" he asked meekly.

"You bet!" Maggot said. He grabbed two corners of the tablecloth and said, "You get those two corners and we'll just lift the whole mess off and set it on the floor."

Earnest looked uncertain, but he grabbed the corners of the cloth and pulled. The dishes wobbled and clinked together, but slowly the cloth sank to the floor without damages.

"Bingo!" Maggot said.

Earnest started spreading books out on the table top. Maggot looked on with growing interest.

"Hey, hey! Motorcycles!" Maggot gasped, reaching for a book. "I didn't know there were books on motorcycles." Already he was fanning through the book, admiring the pictures. "And fishing books! Whooooo! Where did you get all these?" Maggot drooled over the books as if he had just found a new stash of food. "Oh, man, can I borrow these babies?"

"They're yours to keep. Found 'em at rummage sales, mostly. Merry Christmas."

Maggot staggered back and flopped down on a pile of clothes, reading a book on fishing. Earnest sat down beside him and smiled.

"Man, this is great," Maggot said. "How come we don't get any neat books like this at school? All we ever read at school are those boring books on life in Brazil and stuff like that. And ditto sheets. Those stupid, purple ditto sheets that I can't hardly even read."

Earnest chuckled to himself. "Well, let's get started with your first reading lesson."

For an hour the two of them went over and over words. When the lesson was over, the two of them looked like they had been swimming because they were sweating in the warm house.

When Earnest got up to go, he glanced in the box one more time, just to make sure the deodorant and mouthwash were still there, but he said nothing about them. "There are some more books in the box," he said. As he started for the door, Maggot suddenly clomped over to him and wrapped his heavy, sweaty arms tightly around him. "Thanks, Buddy!" he said with a sincere voice. "Thanks a lot."

The hug took Earnest by surprise, but not like the odor that came from Maggot's slippery body. He coughed and pulled away. "Don't worry about it," he said. "Glad to help." Quickly he skipped out the door and down the steps where he took a deep breath of fresh air. He wove his way through the trash to his bike, and soon he was home.

When Earnest strode into the kitchen, it was dark and hot. His parents were sitting at the table looking grim.

"What's up?" Earnest asked.

"The power is off," his father said glumly. "I guess all the air conditioners have overloaded the system." He wiped his forehead with a paper towel.

Earnest sighed. "Oh, fine. What else can go wrong around here?"

Just then the lights came back on.

"Thank God!" Mrs. Wheeler shouted and she jumped up.

Mr. Wheeler staggered to his feet and peered out the window. "You got that right," he said, somberly. And while we are thanking Him, we better put in another request for rain." He shook his head, just thinking about the drought. Then he reached into the pantry and pulled out two plastic buckets. Turning to the sink, he opened the cabinet door and began to unfasten the sink trap.

"What are you doing, Ralph?"

"I'm going to start collecting waste water. If we don't get some water on those new crabapple trees we put out last year, we're going to lose them for sure."

"Why don't you just spray them with the hose?" Earnest asked.

Mr. Wheeler shook his head. "Can't. The city of Mulberry is restricting water. Can't wash your car . . . can't water your plants."

"Oh," Earnest replied. "I didn't know about that."

Mr. Wheeler nodded. "So when you boys take your baths, leave the water in the tub. I'll scoop it out and put it on the trees."

When he had the buckets in place, he trudged outside to the garage and opened the main doors. Then he got into the family car and drove it inside with a roar. The trunk lid flew up when he applied the brakes.

For a few minutes he looked over the old car, then lifted its hood and went to work.

Late that evening he was still working on the car.

7 • Lights On

Mrs. Wheeler was wrapping presents at the kitchen table. The sounds of *Silent Night* rose from the stereo in the living room and filled the entire house.

Sonny staggered in, following the smell of pancakes. His mother quickly hid the presents in the pantry.

"Some silent night," Sonny complained. "Musta been a hundred sirens last night. What happened? Did the whole town burn down, or what?"

Mrs. Wheeler smiled and flipped the pancakes

over. "I know, it sure sounded like it. Just grass fires, I suppose. Everything sounds worse at night."

Sonny slobbered and slurped his orange juice. "Well, tomorrow night is Christmas Eve, and I'm beginning to think maybe Dad and Earnest are right about this Christmas idea. I could really go for a snowstorm or two."

His mother brushed the hair from his eyes.

"Mom, how come we always celebrate Christmas on Christmas Eve instead of Christmas Day, like other people?"

She set a plate of pancakes in front of him. "I don't know. It's always been that way in our family, as far back as I can remember. Is it a problem?"

"Oh, no. In fact, I kinda like it that way. It's easier to think of Jesus in the manger at night time, for some reason."

When he was done with breakfast, Sonny got dressed, then carried a box of old clothes out to the garage. He found two of the wise men had fallen over in the night.

"C'mon, you guys. You are supposed to be smarter than this." He shoved them back up on their feet. "Wise guys! Now, stay put."

He draped a green blanket over the shoulders of one wise man and adjusted it to look like a robe. Satisfied, he dressed the other two wise men, then draped a folded blanket over the camel to look like a saddle.

At last his manger scene was almost finished. "Now, for the final touch," he said to himself. He leaned a ladder against the garage and clambered up it with a hammer in one hand and a homemade wooden star in the other. He stretched out as far as he could reach, trying to center the star on the garage wall. He was almost done nailing when he reached just a little too far.

"Whooooaaaa!" the ladder began to move sideways.

"Eeyyiiiiiii!" Now he was falling through the air. "Helllllp!" On his way down he slammed into one of the wise men, and the other figures began to topple like dominoes as it fell.

"Oof," he hit the grass hands first, then rolled to his side. The camel landed on top of him. He lay there unhurt but embarrassed. A passing car slowed, and the driver stared at Sonny. Sonny jumped up and stared back at him.

At last Sonny had everything back in place. He dusted his hands and looked over the manger set with pride. Just then the star fell to the ground with a *chink*.

Sonny waved his hands in despair. "Forget the star! Who needs stars, anyhow." He was hot and sweaty, so he ambled into the office to cool off.

When he was rested, he jumped to his feet and said, "Now, for the really big shew!" From the storage room he dragged a large cardboard box full of Christmas tree lights. With great effort he hauled the box outside.

"Whatcha doin'?" Cherry asked, coming alongside. She was hiding her head under her sun umbrella.

"You'll see," Sonny said. "You wanna help?"

"Okay, sure. What do I do?"

The two of them carried the box to the front yard and set it down by a large pine tree near the corner of the lot.

Sonny walked around and around the tree, looking it up and down and nodding his head.

"Cherry, my dear, you are looking at the biggest Christmas tree you will ever see in your life."

Cherry shaded her eyes and stared at the huge old tree with its giant pine cones dangling from rugged, massive limbs. "But how you gonna put lights on a tree so tall?"

"Like this!" Sonny shouted. He ran towards the tree and leaped up into the air, catching the lowest limb with both hands. Then he swung his skinny body up on to the limb, straddling it.

"Okay," he shouted. "Start handing me those lights."

It was mid-afternoon before Sonny and Cherry finished stringing the tree with lights.

"These wires look awfully old and scraggly," Cherry noted, as she handed him the last brittle, green wire.

At last Sonny dropped to the ground with a moan and a sigh. "Ohhh, I'm beat. My arms itch, I've got pine oil in my eyes. My hair is all sticky. I sure hope it's worth it." He turned around and admired his work. There was a gleam in his tired eyes as he said, "Cherry, come back at dark and you can watch the big light-up. I'm gonna test 'em out tonight."

By nine o'clock that night it was still not dark, but Sonny grew impatient. "C'mon, everybody," he hollered from the porch. "Let's go. Time to light the tree."

"Big deal," Earnest muttered, putting down his book. "I've seen Christmas trees before," he said, as he trudged out into the yard.

Mr. and Mrs. Wheeler were dressed in their robes and slippers, ready for bed, but they stood near the house to watch.

Cherry helped Sonny hook up the final extension cord from the garage.

"Okay, everybody, this is it!" Sonny stabbed the plug into the socket and heard his mother gasp. "Oh, it's beautiful, simply beautiful."

Sonny smiled a proud smile and looked up at the tree.

Earnest yawned and checked his watch.

For several minutes they admired the bright, multi-colored lights. Passing cars began to slow down and their drivers looked disbelieving at this Christmas tree in July.

The family started to go back into the house when something went wrong. Several bulbs at the base of the tree suddenly went dark. Then a tiny wisp of smoke wriggled up from a small branch.

"Uh-oh."

The finger of smoke was joined by another one, then still another. Now the smoke was joined by a small but bright orange flame.

"Oh, no!"

The small flame grew into a larger flame, and

the larger flame began to spread in both directions around the tree.

What happened next was unexpected. Suddenly the tree seemed to explode with a great roar. The tree turned a brilliant orange color and flames shot upward and outward like powerful torches.

"Call the fire department," Mrs. Wheeler hollered. "And get back, Sonny, get back!"

The drought-dry limbs crackled and hissed as

they boiled into flames. Hot, sticky branches began to drop from the tree, starting little grass fires. Mr. Wheeler dashed to the garage and came streaking back with the garden hose in his hand. Quickly he aimed the stream of water at the little fires, until one by one he had them under control.

Mrs. Wheeler put her hands over her face to keep the blazing heat off of herself. "Cherry, Sonny, Earnest! Get back here, get back here!"

Traffic began to pile up along the road and drivers got out to watch the blaze. They shook their heads and pointed at the fire.

Sonny paced back at forth at a safe distance, mumbling to himself and stopping to kick the ground now and then. Cherry was crying, but she quickly wiped the tears from her cheeks before anyone could notice.

Sirens sounded in the distance, and soon the flicker of fire engine lights glowed against the houses and trees along Morley Highway. By the time the trucks blasted their way onto the lawn, the tree was only a smoldering black shaft against the pink evening sky. Ten minutes from when it started, the fire was all over. The firemen hosed down the tree and most of the lawn in case any sparks were hiding in the dry grass.

Some of Sonny's friends were watching all this from across the road. "Hey, Wheeler!" one of them yelled. "Nice show! What other tricks do you know?" They laughed and whistled, clapped and cheered.

Sonny turned gray in the face. With a growl he turned and kicked his way back to the house. At the porch he stopped and once more looked back at the tree. He pulled back his right foot and kicked the porch lattice so hard it snapped, and a hole appeared where his foot hit. He mumbled something under his breath.

Earnest glared at him, then turned to his father. "Dad! Sonny said a bad word. I heard him."

"I did not."

"Did too!"

"Did not!"

Their father motioned them into the house. "C'mon, both of you. It's all over. Time for bed."

8 • Buggy Ride

"Today is Christmas Eve," Sonny announced at breakfast on Wednesday. The song *Sleigh Ride* was blaring from the stereo, and Mr. Wheeler was tapping his coffee spoon to its beat and singing to himself.

"You see it's lovely weather for a sleigh ride together with you . . ."

Earnest curled his lip and wrinkled his brow. "More like a dune buggy ride," he replied. He pulled off his headphones. "It's already 99 degrees outside." He put his headphones back on.

Mrs. Wheeler pulled a loaf of homemade bread from the oven, when all at once the lights flickered and the room went dark.

"Oh, no, not again," she moaned. "The power is back off. How long this time?"

"Shhh," Earnest said. "I'm listening." In a moment he lifted his headphones and said, "Looks like it's going to be off for two or three hours. According to the news, they're replacing a transformer."

"What?" Mrs. Wheeler yelled. "We can't go three hours without air conditioning. We'll melt like a stick o' butter."

Mr. Wheeler raised an eyebrow. "Why not? We went twenty years without one."

Mrs. Wheeler wiped her hands on a towel and stared angrily out the window. "Some Christmas this is going to be. We might as well just not have one at all."

Mr. Wheeler stood up and tucked in his shirt. "I've got an idea," he said, cheerfully. "Let's go for a drive, down by by river. It's shady out that way and the air conditioning in the car will keep us cool."

"You mean you fixed it?" Earnest asked.

Mr. Wheeler smiled a sneaky smile. "Yep. I

guess now is as good a time as any for my surprise."

"Surprise?" Mrs. Wheeler asked.

He nodded and motioned for the family to follow him. "C'mon, I'll show you."

The boys and their mother followed obediently out to the garage.

"The wind is blowing today," Sonny noted. "Kinda strong."

"That's good," his father replied. "Maybe it will blow in a change of weather. I sure hope so."

"What's the big surprise?" Earnest pressed him.

"Just hold on to your britches." Mr. Wheeler went in the side door of the garage. "You all wait right here."

In a few moments the main garage doors swung up and a car backed out. Mr. Wheeler got out of the car and pointed to it with a proud smile. "Well, what do you think?"

Mrs. Wheeler put her hands to her face and gasped. "Ralph, you got us a new car!"

He shook his head. "Nope. Look again."

"But our car is white, this one is blue."

He patted the roof lovingly. "New paint," he explained. Then he pointed inside the window. "And new upholstery . . . new carpets . . ."

"Oh, Ralph, it's beautiful!"

"Overhauled the engine. New tires, shocks. Fixed the air conditioning." He reached in the open window and twisted a knob. "Even the radio works again." Rock music boomed through the window, and he quickly shut it off.

"So that's what you've been doing out here late at night?"

Mr. Wheeler blushed. "We ought to get three or four more years out of her. I figure we've saved maybe ten thousand dollars, and she's just as good as a new one."

All at once the trunk lid sprang open by itself and dangled in mid air.

"Well, *almost* as good as a new one."

The family climbed into the car, and the new-old Ford headed down the highway to the south. After a while, Mr. Wheeler turned down a gravel road and began to follow the Missouri river through the valley. Huge, old trees hung over the road from both sides, making them feel like they were driving through a tunnel.

"What's that awful smell?" Sonny complained.

Mr. Wheeler pointed to the river bank. "Dead fish. The drought is causing them to lose oxygen in the water." He shook his head in dismay.

On they wove through the trees. Suddenly Mr. Wheeler braked hard to keep from hitting a tree that had fallen across the road.

"Whoops! Road block." The boys got out of the car and helped him move the big tree limbs off the road so they could pass.

"I didn't know the wind was this strong," Sonny said, dragging a big branch off to the side.

"It's not just the wind," his father explained. "It's the drought. These old trees are dying. They need a lot of moisture every day. Truckloads of it."

Back on the road, they soon drove out of the trees and into farm country. They roamed past bean fields and pastures and corn fields. The plants were shriveled and brown. Mr. Wheeler just shook his head and whistled softly between his teeth. "I don't know, Joyce. This is the most serious drought I can remember in my lifetime."

"Look!" Sonny blurted out, pointing up ahead. "What's that drifting across the road? It looks like snow."

"Not snow, *topsoil*," his father said in somber tones. "Pure gold, just blowing away in the wind." He steered the car around one drift after another. "It's turning into a dust bowl," he added.

For an hour no one said anything. They drove

past field after field of ruined crops. Yellowish clouds of dust swirled up in the fields and came rolling across the road, blinding them as they drove through.

As they came over a ridge, Earnest pointed off the the left. "Look! Smoke! Over there!"

Mr. Wheeler braked hard. "Oh, my word, look at that. That poor farmer's pasture is on fire and he's trying to put it out with buckets of water."

Mr. Wheeler started to drive on, but Mrs. Wheeler grabbed him by the wrist. "Wait, Ralph, we can't just drive on and leave him to fight this fire by himself. Can't we do something?"

Mr. Wheeler looked impatient. "Do what, Joyce? This isn't a fire truck. We don't carry water with us. We're miles from the nearest town."

"But we have to do something," she argued. "If that fire isn't put out it could burn down his house and barn!" She leaped out of the car.

"Joyce, what are you doing? Get back here."

Mrs. Wheeler turned around and reached for her floor mat. "C'mon," she shouted to the rest of them. "Get a mat and let's go!"

Mr. Wheeler and the boys followed her, mats in hand. Together they shoved over a fence post so they could get into the field.

Mr. Wheeler began to catch the spirit. "Split up," he ordered. "Just try to keep it from spreading. It's our best hope."

Soon the four of them were pounding the hot, crackling grasses as hard and as fast as they could. As fast as they pounded out the flames, the grass flashed back into orange.

They began to slow down. "It's no use," Mr. Wheeler said. "It's out of control."

Then the wind shifted, blowing the flames back on themselves. "Hurry!" Mrs. Wheeler shouted. "While the wind is right. Maybe we can still stop it." They began to pound harder. The floor mats were smoking and melting in their hands.

Two more cars and a truck stopped behind their car, and soon there were five more neighbors beating at the flames. A tractor suddenly appeared at the hilltop, followed by another smaller one. A young man was driving the larger tractor, and it was pulling a sprayer filled with water. The tractor bounced and roared toward them at full speed. Before long the young man had sprayed a band of water all around the blackened grass.

Plop, plop! car mats slapped at the flames. There were shouts as the firefighters got angry at the fire and beat it back with all their might.

Then, slowly but surely, the fire began to come under control. The wind began to die down. More neighbors arrived with shovels and began to dig around the flames, throwing dirt on what embers remained hidden in the grasses.

At last the fire was out. Only a few trickles of smoke floated up here and there, and they were quickly doused by sharp-eyed neighbors.

The weary neighbors began to gather near the road, so tired they could hardly speak to each other, but the looks in their eyes said it all.

The Wheelers got back in their car, but the farmer waved his hands for them to stop. Sonny and Earnest kicked off their blackened shoes and peeled off their smoky shirts as they waited to see what the farmer wanted.

The old, heavy farmer panted and puffed up to the car and stuck out his rugged hand. "I just want to thank y'all for heppin' me out." His face was lined and smeared with soot and there were tears in his grateful eyes. "You saved my farm . . . saved my life!" he said, over and over again, shaking Mr. Wheeler's hand till he thought it would fall off.

"Just glad to help," Mr. Wheeler replied, and he started to drive away. When he had gone only a few feet, he stuck his head out the window and shouted, "Merry Christmas!"

The farmer stared at him with an odd look and waved uncertainly.

Sonny stuck his head out the back window and shouted, "And a Happy New Year!"

9 • Surprise Gift

When the Wheelers got back from their country ride, the electricity was back on. By the time they had cleaned the smoke and soot off themselves, it was time for a late lunch.

The rest of the afternoon the four of them lounged around the house, trying to regain their strength and get in the mood for Christmas Eve dinner.

The boys at last went outside to look over the car, while their mother began preparing the special Christmas meal.

"How did you do it, Dad?" Sonny asked, testing the trunk lid of the car. "It's really a cool machine, now. Better than when we bought it new."

Mr. Wheeler looked proud of himself. "Necessity is the mother of invention," he said, sounding like a teacher. "When you can't afford something, you do the next best thing."

By four-thirty, Mrs. Wheeler began to set up tables in the yard, under the shade trees. She was humming the tune *I Heard the Bells on Christmas Day* to herself as she worked.

The boys helped her with the tables, then carried out boxes of food and presents, which they stacked on the ground.

"This breeze certainly is a blessing," their mother said, fighting to keep the mint green tablecloth in place with dishes.

Cherry arrived with two plastic buckets full of pink flowers. "These sweet peas are all I could come up with," she explained. "My other flowers all died in the heat."

"Oh, these will be just perfect," Mrs. Wheeler said. "They are truly beautiful, and they'll go with my green tablecloth." She sat the buckets on the picnic tables, and Cherry arranged the sprays of pink. "My grandma says you can't kill sweet peas.

She said if there was a nuclear war, the sweet peas wouldn't even notice."

Mrs. Wheeler laughed, and plucked one sweet pea for her own lapel.

By five-thirty the table was loaded with platters of cold cuts, bowls of sweet-smelling fruit, and ice cream salad. Three kinds of homemade bread perfumed the air with a yeasty smell.

Earnest kept snitching peppernuts from the big bowl, popping them into his mouth, and crunching them hard in his jaws.

Sonny was lighting and tossing firecrackers out in the yard.

At last everything was ready for the special Christmas picnic, and everyone began to gather around the tables. Mr. Wheeler was just starting to say the blessing when someone waved from the driveway.

"Wait for me! Wait up!"

"It's Maggot," Sonny gasped. "Oh, no. Who invited him?"

"*I* did," Earnest fired back.

"Well, hold your noses," Sonny said, pinching his nose with two fingers.

Maggot clomped closer and closer until they could all see there was something different about him. He was wearing clean slacks and shirt, and the shirt was neatly tucked in. His hair was slicked down and his face was shiny and clean. They caught a strong whiff of men's cologne as he took his seat beside them.

"Hey," Sonny whispered, "who's the good-smelling dude?"

Mr. Wheeler said the prayer, then Earnest put a Christmas tape on his boom box and turned it up so all could hear.

The family gorged themselves to the sounds of *Jingle Bells* and *Hark, the Herald Angels Sing*.

"Do you feel like we are being watched?" Cherry asked, pointing to Sonny's wise men, who seemed to be staring at all of them. She chomped into a chocolate-covered pretzel.

"Hey, you wise guys," Earnest shouted. "Don't you know it's not nice to stare at people when they're eating?"

One of the wise men suddenly blew over, falling on his face.

"Serves you right," Earnest quipped.

After the meal, the family exchanged a few presents.

"I got a new watch!" Sonny squealed. "Oh, man, I been wantin' this baby for a long time."

"Thanks for the books," Earnest said, giving his mother a hug.

Cherry played with a set of garden tools the Wheelers bought for her.

"Maggot, what did you get?" Sonny asked.

Maggot held up a fishing rod Earnest had bought for him. He smiled a happy but yellow-toothed smile.

When the gifts were all opened, Earnest reached for a book and handed it to Maggot. Then he stood up and waved his hands for attention.

"Ahem!" he said in a loud voice. "If I may have you-all's attention." The family began to quiet down. Earnest continued. "Maggot has been working on a special present for all of us," Earnest said.

He pointed at Maggot and said, "You're on, Mag. *Do* it."

Maggot staggered to his feet and opened the book to a marked page. The wind played with the pages as he started to read.

"And it . . . it come—came to pass . . . in those days, that there went out a degree—a decree—from Ceezer Gustus . . ."

Sonny smiled to himself, but Earnest hung on every word.

". . . to be taxed with Mary his espo . . . his . . ."

"Espoused," Sonny blurted out. Instantly Earnest rammed an elbow into Sonny's belly. "He doesn't need your help, smart lips," Earnest growled into Sonny's ear.

Maggot went on. "And so it was that, that, that, while they were there, the, the days were uh comp, uh something that she should be de-livered."

"They cut her liver out?" Sonny mumbled. Earnest frowned at him.

Maggot took a deep breath, licked his upper lip and read on. "And she, and she brought first her fourth-born son, and wra, wrapped him in swad uh ling clothes, and laid him in a manger . . ."

"Brought *forth* her *first*born," Sonny whispered, "*not* brought first her forthborn, for pity sakes."

With tight lips Earnest whispered in Sonny's ear, "How would you like to be the first to *die* in our family?"

There was a flicker of light in the distant sky, but no one noticed it.

"I bring you good tidings of of gra-great joy," Maggot read on.

Suddenly a powerful gust of cool wind lifted the

tablecloth right in their faces, and the sweet peas sailed out of the buckets and went tumbling across the lawn. Everyone stuck out his arms to hold the tablecloth in place.

Maggot went on reading, raising his voice to be heard over the wind. "And sudden. . . suddenly there was with the the angels a hevly host praising, praising God and saying, 'Glory to God in the the highest.'"

All at once the wind blasted them in the face so hard they nearly fell off their seats. At the same time the earth and sky exploded like a hundred sonic booms all at one time.

"LOOK!" Mr. Wheeler shouted. "RAIN! It's going to rain! Look at that sky! Look at those clouds!"

Mrs. Wheeler dived for the tables and caught them just before they both blew over. "Help me!" she screamed, but the others were dancing around the yard and pointing at the flashing, booming clouds in the north.

Mr. Wheeler stood quietly, reverently, staring into the sky. The wind toyed with his hair and dried the tears that streamed down his cheeks. "Praise God," he mumbled, over and over. "Praise God."

Large drops of rain hit the ground with a loud smack, then a steady mist of finer rain began to soak them through and through.

"Somebody please help me!" Mrs. Wheeler called out, and the boys dashed to her rescue. Together they carried food and plates to the kitchen, stopping along the way to admire the coiling black clouds that crept across the sun. Soon their hair was matted down and their clothes clung to them, but they were singing.

"Rain . . . rain . . . rain, I love the rain," the boys chanted, as they ran back and forth, back and forth.

Craaaaack, booom BOOOOM! A big bolt of lightning struck nearby and the boys leaped on to the porch with a yelp.

"MERRY CHRIST-MAS!" Sonny yelled at the top of his lungs.

10 • And the Winner Is . . .

For two hours the Wheelers sat on the porch, watching the rain. Maggot and Sonny kept dashing off the porch and into the rain with squeals of joy. Then they dashed back, whenever the lightning struck nearby.

"The air feels so good," Mrs. Wheeler said with a long sigh. "I have forgotten what it feels like to be cool."

Earnest was listening intently to his walkman. He pulled off his headphones and said, "Well, it looks like the drought is going to end. The jet stream is turning south, pulling cool air down from Canada."

Mr. Wheeler just hummed to himself, admiring the wind and clouds. "It's too late for the crops," he said, "but the farmers might get in a second crop if they hurry."

The rain slowed a little. Earnest and Cherry finally dared to join Maggot and Sonny, sloshing through deep puddles in the yard. They laughed and pushed each other, falling down and crawling through the cool water like porpoises.

"You know," Mr. Wheeler said, "that looks like so much fun I wish I was a kid again." He staggered to his feet and kicked off his shoes.

"Ralph, what are you doing?" Mr. Wheeler never answered. He peeled off his socks and rolled up his pants legs. He padded barefoot down the porch steps and sloshed his way out into the deepest puddle. Reaching down, he began slapping the water at Sonny, and Sonny slapped it back at him with a squeal. Soon all of them were spraying each other in every direction.

Sonny stopped and looked up at the porch. "C'mon in, Mom," he yelled, but she folded her arms and shook her head stubbornly.

"C'mon, Joyce. Lighten up!"

But Mrs. Wheeler stood up and turned to go into the house.

"Let's get her!" Mr. Wheeler shouted. The boys leaped out of the puddle and raced behind their father. The three of them grabbed Mrs. Wheeler by the arms. She shrieked and screamed.

"Ralph! Stop! No! Don't do this! I don't want to get wet!" They tugged at her, but she fought back. "You'll be sorry, Ralph, I mean it! Don't do this! I'll never forgive you in a million years! Eeeeeeeeeeeek! Let go of me, you brutes, you're hurting me!"

She tried to hold on to the porch posts, but the boys pried her hands away and pulled her down the steps. She kicked and sputtered, but the boys were winning. "Stop this right now, I mean it!"

Cherry muffled her giggles as she watched the boys drag Mrs. Wheeler into the puddles.

"Ralph, no, please, I don't *like* water. I'll drown. No, I'll drown *you!*"

At last she was in the middle of the puddle and the boys let go of her. Mr. Wheeler kicked water on her and she glared at him.

With fire in her eyes, she reached out and grabbed her husband and pulled so hard he fell on his face in the puddle. There he lay, laughing and begging for mercy, as she showered him over and over with spray. The boys helped her.

"Ralph Wheeler, you will pay for your crime, if I have to put poison in your lunch."

By eight-thirty the first wave of rain had passed, but more clouds were building in the west.

The family sat dripping and happy on the porch. Mrs. Wheeler passed around a platter of chocolate-covered pretzels and the bowl of peppernuts.

"You know," she said in a wistful voice, "this is one of the nicest Christmases I remember."

"Let's have it in July every year," Sonny said. "Who needs snow, anyhow?"

"When are we gonna have the judging?" Earnest wanted to know.

"Oh, that's right," Mrs. Wheeler replied. "I almost forgot about our contest."

For several minutes they discussed the presents they had given and received.

"I give the prize to Earnest," Maggot said. "He gave me a whole truckload of great books . . . and taught me how to read better."

Earnest blushed.

"And how to use deodorant," Sonny whispered to Cherry, who giggled.

"What about Sonny's manger scene?" Mr. Wheeler said. "And his Christmas tree. That was certainly the brightest tree I've seen in a long time." He winked at Sonny, and Sonny hung his head.

"Joyce, your Christmas picnic was truly a meal to remember. It even *looked* beautiful."

She looked pleased with her husband's praise. "I'm just glad I was smart enough to marry a man who knows how to fix things."

A pickup truck drove slowly by the house. It stopped and turned around in a nearby driveway, then slowly drove by the house again. The driver kept looking up toward the Wheeler's house. Once more the truck turned anround and drove past the house and pulled in another driveway.

"Somebody lost?" Mrs. Wheeler wondered out loud.

"Probably just can't get enough of my manger set," Sonny boasted.

"Yeah, right," Earnest replied, sarcasm in his voice.

"It's coming back again. He's stopping. Boys, don't stare!"

"Well, *you're* staring, "Earnest piped up.

The old truck hestitated at the Wheeler garage,

then turned into the driveway towards them. Mrs. Wheeler jumped up. "We can't have company looking like this. We're a mess." She started into the house.

"Relax, Joyce. Probably just someone needing directions."

The pickup truck scrunched to a standstill a few yards away. An old man staggered out and reached back inside for something. Slowly he made his way up the drive to the Wheelers. He was dressed in a nice shirt and slacks with a colonel tie dangling crookedly from his neck.

The man stood at the porch steps and smiled. He held out his hand to Mr. Wheeler and said, "I believe I have a little something for you folks."

Mr. Wheeler shook the man's hand. "Have we met before?" he asked the old man.

"Well, I guess so!" the old man said with a chuckle and a twinkle in his eye. "Just this morning. My name's McClurg. Robert McClurg."

Mr. Wheeler studied the face carefully, but in vain.

The old man smiled. "You may have forgotten me, but I'll never forget you folks. 'Course I didn't look the same as I look right now."

Suddenly Mr. Wheeler recognized the man.

"Oh, yes! Of course! You're the farmer whose field was on fire!"

The old man smiled and held out a heavy paper sack. "I just brought you a little something to express my thanks for what you did."

Mr. Wheeler peered in the sack.

"There's a couple dozen eggs in there and some steaks on the bottom. It's not much, but it's my way of saying how much I appreciated what you all did."

"Well, you are certainly welcome, but how did you find us?"

"My grandson recognized one o' your boys, from a basketball game." The man turned and started for his truck. "Thanks again," he hollered over his shoulder.

"Thank you!" Mr. Wheeler shouted after him. "You didn't have to do this!"

The old man waved and climbed into his truck.

Mrs. Wheeler came back outside when the man was gone. "What was that all about?" she wanted to know.

Mr. Wheeler handed her the sack of food. "That was the farmer we helped out this morning when his field was on fire."

"Well, how nice of him."

Earnest looked impatient. "Let's get on with the judging," he said. "Who wins the prize for the best gift?"

Everyone turned and looked at Cherry. She blushed and put her hand under her chin and looked deep in thought. Suddenly she pointed up to the sky and said, "I give the prize to God . . . for the rain!"

"Yeah, me too," Sonny said.

"Me too," Earnest agreed. The others nodded their agreement.

"Good choice, Cherry," Mrs. Wheeler added.

Mr. Wheeler hugged her and said, "You are a good judge. Thanks to God this is one of the best Christmases I can remember." He stopped and stared out at the garage. "Look!" he shouted. "*They* think so too!"

Everyone turned and looked at Sonny's manger set. The serious magazine faces had come loose in the rain and they had fallen to the ground, leaving the big smiling faces staring at them.

Sonny chuckled to himself. "See, Earnest, God likes my faces better. So there."

Wheeler's Adventures

Wheeler's Treasure

Sonny and Earnest search for treasure in an old abandoned mining town near Mulberry.

Wheeler's Special Gift

The Wheelers celebrate Christmas in July. Who can give the best Christmas gift?

Wheeler's Swap

After Sonny and Earnest show their cousin Buddy the good things about small-town life, he brings them to his home in New York City.

Wheeler's Big Move

The brothers try to change their father's mind about moving away from Mulberry.